Mr. Bennet's Illness

A Short Farce

By Timothy Underwood

I would like to thank my beta readers Steeleo, Betty Jo, Brooke Till, MandieS1978, and my sister who also loved the story. DJ Hendrickson edited the book. Thank you everyone, I appreciate the help greatly.

Mr. Bennet's Illness

At the time Mr. Bingley arrived at Netherfield, Mr. Bennet was in the process of recovering from a serious illness. He had very nearly died, and the high fever had left him unusually sensitive to noise.

Noise. Noise. Noise.

"You must call on Mr. Bingley. You must call on Mr. Bingley. You must call on Mr. Bingley."

Couldn't she see he was trying to read?

"Oh! My dear, what a fine thing for our girls! I am thinking of his marrying one of them."

"Why would he ever wish to marry? Wives and children are so much noise."

Mrs. Bennet ignored the hint. "Nonsense! How can you talk so? We are so very happy together. And none of our children are very noisy, except Lizzy."

"Lizzy is the only one of the lot who ever has anything sensible to say."

"It is very likely that Mr. Bingley may fall in love with one of our girls, and therefore you must visit him as soon as he comes."

"You and the girls may go yourselves." She'd ignored his last hint. Maybe he should say the opposite of what he hoped her to do. Manipulate the fragile psyche of a woman by reverse. "You should not go with them, for you are as handsome as any of the girls, and Mr. Bingley may like you the best of the party."

Yesssss, run off with Mr. Bingley, and never talk to me again! Hahahaha. I shall read my books in peace.

"My dear, you flatter me. I certainly have had my share of beauty, but at my age a woman ought to give over thinking of her own beauty."

Damn. "Most women at your age have not much beauty to think of. You are so beautiful that he would immediately fall in love with you and convince you to leave me and travel the continent with him, living in decadent sin. I would be alone and only have my books for company. Don't do that to me."

"Hahahaha. Heavens, what a teasing notion!" She patted him on the shoulder. "But, my dear, you must go and see Mr. Bingley when he comes to the neighborhood."

"Had we not decided that you and the girls would go by yourselves?"

"Consider your daughters. You must go, for it will be impossible for us to visit him if you do not."

It would be at least twenty minutes to Netherfield, another twenty to listen to this Bingley, and then twenty back. He'd lose an hour he could spend reading. Unacceptable.

"You are over-scrupulous, surely. I dare say Mr. Bingley will be very glad to see you."

"Oh! You take delight in vexing me. You have no compassion for my poor nerves."

Her nerves; her nerves; her nerves. Did she never talk about anything else? Ever? To think they once amused him. How? So much noise. So much. And it was harder to read when she was in a nervous flutter.

Mrs. Bennet continued, "Ah, you do not know what I suffer. For those who never complain never are respected."

"You never complain. Hahahahahaha."

Mrs. Bennet was not nearly so amused. With a frown she begged Mr. Bennet again. "Do promise you shall visit Mr. Bingley."

"Shall you be silent for the next two hours entire if I make such a promise?"

"Oh, yes! My dear, yes. You are the best of fathers. An exemplary husband. Your daughters are so very lucky —"

"Fine, I'll go. Just be silent."

Mrs. Bennet sat there quietly. There was a quivering tension in her manner that proclaimed a desire to speak again. Mr. Bennet tried to ignore it and focus on the Greek letters on the page in front of him. But there was an ache in the back of his neck that proclaimed he would be interrupted the instant he relaxed into reading.

Mmm. Plato. Philosopher kings. A metaphor comparing women and men to dogs. Plato thought women were just as good as men, except physically weaker. Ha. The great philosopher was wrong on that. Bitches barked louder.

The door was slammed open violently, and the windows shook with the force.

"La!" Lydia hopped into the room and jumped up and down enthusiastically.

Mr. Bennet winced. He stared resolutely at the text of *The Republic*. Maybe if he pretended she was not there, Lydia would dissolve into an ether.

"It is such great news! Mrs. Phillips told me! You must hear it. You Must Hear It!"

"Be *quiet*, I *attempt* to read."

"Papa, Papa! A regiment is to be quartered in Meryton! A militia regiment!" Lydia danced and twirled on the floor. The dull thuds pounded through Mr. Bennet's skull each time she landed. "I shall be so handsome, and they shall all wear red coats, and I will flirt with every officer and one shall marry me! It will be such a joke when I am married before Jane."

"Aye, it shall be great fun!" cried Mrs. Bennet. "But you must *only* flirt with the penniless officers. But mayhap the colonel is unmarried and will take a liking to you."

"Not unless he is remarkably stupid." Mr. Bennet grunted from his chair. The fire was warmer here, but he would go to his study where he could be surrounded by his walls and piles of books.

Lydia replied, "La! You are so funny, Papa! An officer stupid! Such a joke. Hahahahaha! Why they are the cleverest and best dressed class of gentlemen in England. I am determined I shall only marry an officer."

"If there are no stupid officers, your aim shall not succeed. More's the pity."

*****

A week after Mr. Bingley arrived at Netherfield Mr. Bennet at last forced himself away from the tantalizing stream of endless words in his study. For the first time in more than a week he buttoned himself up into a tailcoat and wrapped his cravat around his neck, still conscious of his recently recovered health.

Mr. Bennet stood in the dusty, smelly, animal infested barn and waited while the groom saddled the horse and tightened the straps around its girth. Mr. Bennet then mounted with a disgusted sigh.

He could be reading.

It was a dreary day, but then all days in England were dreary. He would enormously prefer to be indoors reading. The clop of his horse's hooves was loud and irritating. When he rode through Meryton, people called out greetings and shouted demands to buy things.

He wanted quiet.

Mr. Bennet settled onto the road straight out to Netherfield and he began to think.

He had nearly died. Such a happenstance made a man think more seriously on his life and future. He did not know how much longer he might have. It was time he should focus on those matters that were most important.

Books.

There were so many books.

And they published more every year!

Each time he looked at the beauties of Plato, Virgil, Aquinas and Samuel Richardson they grew anew for him. Would Clarissa mysteriously die of a violated virtue every time he read the novel? Would the philosopher kings rule the imaginary state of Atlantis every time? Was it still possible to answer all questions under heaven and earth?

He must read them all.

Read *all* the books.

Time was passing, and he wasted it on these trivial, unimportant matters, like trying to marry off his daughters and listen to his wife.

If only he could get rid of his daughters, especially Lydia. It would be so much quieter. He could encourage Mrs. Bennet to call on them all the time and take her noise elsewhere. It would be only him and his books. A perfect life.

Maybe marrying his daughters off *wasn't* a trivial, unimportant task. He'd get rid of all of them except Elizabeth, who sometimes said clever things.

Mr. Bingley was a jolly loud fellow who greeted Mr. Bennet with an effusive handshake and a shouted, "Hello, hello. It is deuced fine to meet you. Deuced fine!"

Mr. Bingley grinned. He stood in the light, handsome and young, with curly reddish hair and a fine silk waistcoat. He looked like a remarkably stupid fellow. Mr. Bennet loathed him. He would do excellently for one of his girls, especially Lydia.

"There is no chance you ever were an officer?"

Bingley blinked and shook his head. "Not at all. Not at all. It was Cambridge for me. Met some deuced good friends there, especially Darcy. He'll be down for a visit later this month. It was a fine time! Deuced fine. I hear you are a scholar. I daresay you had a fine time at university."

"So never an officer. Pity. Well, you'll do for one of the others. My wife wishes you to know that you can marry any of my girls you wish. For my part I'd rather you don't marry Lizzy since she is clever, and you seem like a nattering fool. And Lydia has sworn to only marry an officer, I'll find one for her when the regiment arrives. As for the others, they are all loud mouthed louts, like you. You'll get along splendidly."

Mr. Bingley looked more than a little offended at this speech. "I assure you, sir, I am not here to find a wife."

"Oh? My wife was convinced that was your aim in settling. Well, maybe you are cleverer than you sound. Don't ever marry; it is a recipe for noise, noise, noise. They never quiet down and let a man read. Never. I've not been able to sink into my darling books for years. You though are a very loud fellow yourself, so you don't need much quiet, I suspect. Would you like to run off with my wife?"

Bingley laughed uncomfortably, pretending to take the offer as a joke. "You are very singular, Mr. Bennet."

"I've been told *that* before. Well I've done my duty now. My wife can't complain I didn't call on you. Do think about my daughters, I would dearly like to never hear them again. Except Lizzy, she is a clever girl. Do you happen to know any clever men?"

"Well, my friend Darcy."

"Excellent, does he talk much?"

"No, never. He is quite a silent fellow with those he doesn't like. I dare say you two would get along fabulously."

"I doubt that. I get along well with no one. Especially my family. They are so loud. Have I mentioned I hate noise?"

"You have."

"I despise every sound. The creak of the house, the crackling of the fire, the clop of horses. Servants bustling about. But worst of all are my wife and daughters. 'La, Heavens, Such a Joke, do this my dear, do that, go speak to that rich new man. Stop reading and attend to me.' Never marry — unless it is to take one of my daughters. They are a noisy bunch."

With that Bingley and Bennet shook hands and the call ended. Half an hour later Mr. Bennet was in his study happily reading Burke's *Reflections on the Revolution in France*. Burke was right to dislike the revolution. It made an awful lot of noise.

*****

Mr. Bingley's amiability and good nature was such that he did return Mr. Bennet's call. When Mr. Bingley was brought by the quiet servant into Mr. Bennet's study, Bingley stepped forward towards his host with his hand out wide and exclaimed, "Zounds, you've a fine pile here. It's blasted good to see you again, Bennet."

Mr. Bennet winced and startled. "Must you always be so loud?"

He stood, holding his book in his left hand, with a finger in it to keep his place, and desultorily shook Bingley's hand. "I'm near the best part of Aquinas's *Summa*. I cannot stop turning the pages once I'm deep into it — listen to this, 'whether delight is in time? Objection one: It would seem that delight is in time. For delight is a kind of movement, as the Philosopher says. But all movement is in time. Therefore delight is in time. *On the contrary,* The Philosopher says that 'no one takes pleasure according to time.' I answer that a thing may be in time in two ways: first, by itself; secondly, by reason of something else, and accidentally as it were. For since time is the measure of success of things — "

"Yes — yes. Bennet, I believe I understand. Very fascinating. Very. You need not read the whole argument to me."

"Are you certain? I am moved near to tears each time I read it. I hope you do not mind if I sit down and continue." Mr. Bennet generously waved his hand in a large circle to indicate the stuffed bookshelves around the room. "There's plenty you might read for yourself."

"Yes, certainly."

Without further ado, Mr. Bennet sat down and began to read again. Bingley shrugged and looked around. Maybe Darcy and Bennet would get along well. He would need to bring his friend calling. Darcy was entertained by singular characters. Bingley sat and tried to read, but he was mostly wondering about the pretty girls he had heard were Mr. Bennet's daughters. Should he ask to see if they could be introduced? Bennet had said he wanted very much for them to be married. Bingley decided against it. Mostly because Bennet looked frightening in the intensity with which he read his book. He worried that the man might do something vicious if interrupted again.

Matters proceeded much as they did in Jane Austen's version of this tale: Bingley was entranced at the assembly by the angelic beauty of Jane Bennet, while Mr. Darcy insulted Elizabeth, which happily distracted her from worrying over the changes in her father's personality since his illness. She immediately determined that she loathed the arrogant man.

Upon their return from the assembly, Mr. Bennet, like in Austen's tale, exclaimed with passion that he wished Bingley had sprained his ankle on the first dance, so he did not need to hear of his partners. And, like in Austen's tale, Mr. Bennet absolutely refused to hear a description of the lace upon Mrs. Hurst's gown.

However, he did not hear of Mr. Darcy's shocking rudeness, as after exclaiming against a description of finery, Mr. Bennet stood and retreated to his study where he could commune with the endless pages in peace.

Mr. Bingley did take Darcy to call upon Mr. Bennet, and the two did in fact get along like whisky and a drunkard. Or at least as well as two gentlemen who read together in the same room, but almost never spoke, could be said to get along.

Mr. Darcy called at Longbourn quite often and would sit with Mr. Bennet enjoying his expansive library for an hour at a time. Darcy enjoyed Mr. Bennet's company enormously more than that of Sir Lucas, or Mr. Goulding, or any of the other self-important fools of the neighborhood. That he had opportunity to speak to and see the handsome and lively Miss Elizabeth when he called on Mr. Bennet was only, Darcy resolutely affirmed to himself every time he visited, a secondary draw.

Like in Austen's tale, Jane rode to Netherfield in the rain and
became sick. Elizabeth followed her sister and, depending
upon your interpretation of the tale, spent the next days
flirting with or arguing angrily with Mr. Darcy. She returned
from Netherfield as convinced as ever that she loathed Mr.
Darcy.
Even though her increasingly eccentric father considered him
to be a fine, quiet fellow.
It is at this point that the hero of our story arrives, clad in
sweat and fat.
Mr. William Collins was a man sent forth by a noble lady
upon a mission. He must find a wife, ideally from amongst his
lovely cousins. And so he would. He rather viewed himself in
the nature of a dragon slayer, St. George, off to nobly bring the
deepest of happiness unto a deserving woman, who would
thus save her family from destitution upon the death of their
father.
Mr. Collins was a man of short, rather than middling height.
He had an ample, almost feminine bosom, and his hair was
quite greasy. Lady Catherine believed that frequent bathing
was the cause of the decline of the Roman Empire, and as a
result Mr. Collins had chosen not to bathe once in the past six
months. He covered up the smell by the application of copious
amounts of cologne that went before him declaring his
presence like a band of trumpeters.
Upon his disembarking with his trunk from the hired carriage,
Mr. Collins was met with a vision of such astonishing
loveliness that he knew at once his fate was forevermore
settled.

He stared gape mouthed at the tall (taller than he, certainly) angel who came towards him, with a sparkling smile and a pink ribboned straw bonnet. He stumbled forward to speak to her. "Oh, ye creature who sparkles brightly in the sun" — Mr. Collins considered it his place as a clergyman to presume upon speaking to anyone, especially a delectable maiden of delight, without introduction — "tell me, are you, is it possible, perhaps might I hope that you are amongst the enumerated order of my cousins?"

A high pitched giggle — such a lovely, lovely sound — was the reply.

Mr. Collins took this reply as an affirmative. "Lady, whose beauty shines forth from every ribbon and lace upon your person, lead me unto your noble and beneficent parents!"

"La, you are so dull." She dismissively waved her delicate fingers, thus crushing the heart of our perspiring hero. She opened the door and yelled indiscriminately into the house, "Lizzy, Mama, everyone, our Cousin Collins is here. And he's ugly! He'll stink up the whole house."

And the call returned from the house: "Lydia! Be silent you silly, ignorant girl! Noise! Noise! Noise! That is all you ever make. I'm reading!"

And with this introduction, Mr. Collins was led into the house that would one day be ruled over by him and the vision of loveliness, who was so blinded by her own appearance that she rightly claimed that everyone else was ugly, even Mr. Collin's upright and manly form — praised twice by Lady Catherine herself. And further Mr. Collins's appearance had been complimented once by a woman of ill repute attempting to weasel his treasured virginity from him via true flattery. The harlot failed, of course. Mr. Collins would proudly tell anyone that he today was yet untouched by a woman since the day his mother died.

It had only come to pass those three times that others had spoken of how fine looking Mr. Collins was in his presence, but he knew there were many more occasions when he was not there that women discoursed upon his fashionable and masculine appearance, for in general women found it impossible to look upon him or meet him in the eyes. That was a sure sign of their overpowering attraction for his form.

The attraction of women to him had mightily intensified since he ceased to bathe upon Lady Catherine's advice.

During dinner Elizabeth was amused by the ridiculousness of Mr. Collins's character — I am forced to confess that our favorite Bennet daughter did not admire the blubbered hero of this tale as you and I do.

Mr. Bennet was torn between amusement at his character, and hatred of the man whose endless speaking prevented him from properly attending to the book he kept in his left hand as the rest of the family spoke, flipping the pages in between bites, after carefully wiping his fingers off upon the cloth napkins.

After dinner was completed, they went to the drawing room. Mr. Bennet felt obliged, since this was a man who he might be able stuff one of the noisy brood upon, to follow with them, though he would much rather read *alone*. Then a happy thought occurred to Mr. Bennet.

"Mr. Collins, would you not read to us from a book? The ladies do not read overmuch themselves, but this is a way for them to access printed words that matches the deficiency of my family's — I except Lizzy in this insult — learning. They require noise. Constant, unending noise. So it would be greatly to my liking if you would indulge their need for noise with a book."

"I am most honored by the request to read! I can see you are a
scholar of great note. My father never read much, and I am
very, very, very willing to be guided by you on which books
to read. Lady Catherine believes that a clergyman should be
both learned and practical, like the Apostle Paul, able to earn
his bread through tentmaking and a scholar — not to imply
that the apostle Paul was not a gentleman, I am sure he did
not *need* to dirty his hands, and only made tents as a pastime. *I
myself never make any tents—*"

"Jove! I care not!"

"And Lady Catherine insists that a clergyman should have the
competence to emposition an immoderate amount of allusions
in his sermons, and—"

"Yes, yes, yes." God! Even when the man was going to read a
book, he made so much noise about it. "Just pick a book. *Any
book.*"

A book was handed to him by Kitty. Mr. Collins looked upon
it and recoiled, "Good God! A novel!" It seemed as though the
white line of his clerical collar choked his bulging and
protruding neck fat. "I never read novels."

Of course he didn't. This terrible man did not appreciate
books. That was why he was so noisy. Mr. Bennet *really* hoped
he took one of his daughters, else this evening would be
entirely wasted.

Lizzy and Jane grabbed other books from the shelves, and
displayed them for him. He happily picked Fordyce's
Sermons, and opened to a passage from the middle: "In
Modest Apparel, as opposed to that which is Indecent, and to
that which is Vain: Distinctions, whereof the theory, I must
confess, it is in many cases not easy, and in some perhaps not
practicable, to settle with precision; such a powerful influence
in those matters have custom and the opinions of the world.
But in this instance, as in others where the passions are
concerned, the strictest-casuist will—"

Mr. Collins paused with a wrinkled forehead, as though he wanted to figure out what "strictest-casuist" meant. Mr. Bennet knew neither, and he did not care. He was as near to heaven he could be without reading directly himself. He loved the written word, even when it was the spoken word, no matter what the topic. Perhaps in the future the artificers of men would develop such devices as could speak books directly to men, and he could leave that speaking whilst he slept, and thus make books to fill his dreams without the bother of a servant burning a candle and speaking from the corner of his bedroom.

"I presume, be generally the safest." Mr. Collins continued with a flat, monotonous voice that lacked the enthusiasm and joy that reading should bring. "The zeal of the ancient Fathers on such subjects carried some of them far; farther, I doubt, than the relaxation of modern manners would well bear. Were a young woman now a days, from a peculiar — "

"Do you know, Mama, that my Uncle Phillips talks of turning away Richard, and if he does, Colonel Forster will hire him." Mr. Bennet stared with something much like hate at his youngest daughter, as she interrupted the glorious flow of words.

Jane and Lizzy — good girls both of them, bid Lydia to be quiet. *Yes, never say anything!*

Mr. Collins however laid aside his book and said, "I have often observed how little young ladies are interested by books of a serious stamp. Such a creature of loveliness such as Cousin Lydia—" He lingered over the tones of her name in a way reminiscent to how Mr. Bennet's voice lingered over the word *books*. "—needs no such instruction on modesty — for she is always modesty — nor on ornamentation, for her hair and cheeks and nose… and her bosom and all her other female attributes are ornamentation enough for her, and the intrinsic wisdom of her good sense, and malleability of her character will ensure she uses good judgement when she chooses how to adorn herself, and she will—"
"Just read!"
"Nay," Mr. Collins replied, bestowing a singularly repellent toad-like smile on Lydia — Mr. Bennet thought he might vomit — "I will not importune my sweet, young cousin. Rather, Mr. Bennet, I would happily serve you as an antagonist at backgammon." Mr. Collins offered this game to his host as he had suddenly recollected overhearing in a conversation between two other gentlemen at university that a man must not pay too much attention to a Lady early in their acquaintance, lest he seem desperate. And he was desperate for Lovely Lydia's approval.
"No," Mr. Bennet replied coldly. "I will do no such thing with a man who ceases to read a book for any reason. I have been too long away from my dearest, most precious treasures, and I must return to them in my study, lest they become cold and lonely."
And with that Mr. Bennet left the room, took up a new book as soon as he entered his study, and lived for the next hours as happily as a happy and rational man could ever hope to live.

*****

The next morning Mr. Collins and Mrs. Bennet had a rendezvous, when Mr. Collins extended unto the mother of his Lovely Lydia the information that he had come unto them with the intention of making the offer of his, elevated by the beneficence of Lady Catherine de Bourgh, hand to one of his dear cousins so that he might spare the family of unhappiness and stress at that time, which he hoped most assiduously would be in the great distant future, for he would not wish Lovely Lydia to suffer — Cousin Lydia, he meant, for it was too soon to speak of her on such familiar and intimate pettish terms — from the death of a beloved parent. And that further he had settled his inclination most decidedly the moment he first saw *her*.

Mrs. Bennet turned to stir the fire in the breakfast room as she considered his communication. On the one hand she welcomed a man of Mr. Collins's expectations as a husband for any of her girls. Except Jane who had better prospects. On the other hand...

Lydia stuck her head in the breakfast room and saw Mr. Collins standing in conference next to her mother. She exclaimed, "La! Mr. Collins is down already. What a joke, but he is much too dull to speak to! I shall far rather to find a bite in the kitchen."

And with that the sublime vision of heavenly perfection disappeared from Mr. Collins's blinded eyes, and the sound of angelic choirs singing in heaven ceased in his benumbed ears. It was many seconds before he shook himself from the stupefaction which Lydia's presence brought.

Mrs. Bennet knew her favorite needed a more entertaining husband than Mr. Collins, and she thought Lydia would refuse him in any case.

"Yes, well," Mrs. Bennet said, straightening up. "You would do much better I think to choose one of the other girls. Perhaps Lizzy, she is the prettiest except Jane."

"Nay, my inclinations are carved in stone, like the tablets which Moses brought down unto the people of Israel after he had communed with God in the mountains and which he threw down and smashed upon seeing the sins of the Israelites — I mean like the other stone tablets. The ones he didn't smash. My inclination is as undoable as the Gordian knot, which Alexander the Great cut — I mean..." Mr. Collins ceased to speak as he hunted about in his mind for a classical allusion which did not involve something that clearly *could* be undone. "My inclinations are like the—"

"You and Lydia would not suit," Mrs. Bennet interrupted him. "My youngest is decidedly enthusiastic about officers and red coats and soldierly men. Not white collars." She shook her head discouragingly. "Nor white colors. She needs interesting conversation, and well... she finds you dull."

"Of course she does not. My position in life and my connection to the great Lady Catherine de Bourgh are such that no lady of my sweet, delectable, tasty cousin's station in life could find me dull."

"She said so directly," Mrs. Bennet replied with a touch of asperity.

"Ahhh, my dear hostess. Though you are her mother, and a woman yourself, it seems you are ignorant of the usual practices of elegant females. Female delicacy is such that they pretend indifference to the man who they secretly admire. She means to increase my love by suspense. Which she succeeds at doing, though my situation in life, and my connections with the family of de Bourgh, and my relationship to your own, are circumstances so highly in my favor that I can feel no true suspense."

Mrs. Bennet stared at him. For once in her life she was struck speechless, a feat her husband, to his great disappointment, had never succeeded upon. At last she ventured, in a small voice, "I really think you would do better to marry Lizzy than Lydia."

"Why are we talking about marriage to Lizzy?" Mr. Bennet
had walked in through the open door to the breakfast room, a
thick book held up in front of his nose. He spoke without
putting it down as he grabbed a roll from the table with his
free hand. "Her and Mr. Collins would not suit, despite my
longing for an empty study room, I would not give my
blessing to such a match."

"Mournlessly I do not mourn that." Mr. Collins replied, "I
have attached an attachment to your sweet, delectable, tasty,
lovely Lydia. She is all that is charm and perfection, and I only
must secure her attachment to me to achieve complete and
final happiness — and your approval, dear cousin, which I ask
now in hopes that you look in favor upon attaching my
attachment for life."

Mr. Bennet finished chewing and swallowed his roll, and he
lowered his book. "Certainly you shall marry Lydia — she has
had no luck in the three weeks since the regiment has arrived
in marrying one of the officers. That was enough time. I assure
you, I shall make her marry. But what was that talk of Lizzy?"

"My dear, think about it — Lydia would not make a good
clergyman's wife. She is too lively and uncontrolled. She
would not show your patroness proper deference, Mr. Collins.
And… Lizzy is much prettier than Lydia. She would make a
far superior clergyman's wife. Lizzy reads a great deal —
Lydia takes after me. I am not even certain that she can read."

Mr. Collins replied solemnly. "It is not a given to woman to
read. There is no need. Her form is perfection itself, I wish
nothing else."

"By Gad, Mrs. Bennet," Mr. Bennet spoke. "You mean to say
you did not teach Lydia to read! No wonder she talks so
much. Mr. Collins, I assure you, Lydia would make a perfect
clergyman's wife — you have my full and hearty blessing."

"The life of a clergyman's wife is so quiet. My Lydia needs
noise, and stimulation, and clothes, and pretty things. She
likes officers."

"I assure you, it is not contrary to the nature of a clergyman to be loud. A clergyman must be loud every Sunday as he preaches his sermon to his devout congregation. I can be as loud as the voice of God speaking to John the Baptist as he baptized our savior…" Mr. Collins realized this allusion could be construed as blasphemous, so he hurriedly added, "Me and your Lydia are a perfect match."

Mr. Bennet nodded enthusiastically and picked up his book once more. "He certainly can be loud."

"Yes, but she can be impertinent — do you not think Lizzy would be a much better wife? She knows when to be quiet."

"I cannot wish quietness; I wish my perfect sweet noisy Lydia."

Mrs. Bennet sighed theatrically. "Oh my nerves, my nerves. I shall attempt to convince her — but you would much prefer one of the other girls. Especially Lizzy."

Mr. Bennet left and entered his library. He looked at his happy books. They surrounded him, a warm comforting wall of books. Mr. Bennet began to cackle.

"Soon. Soon." Mr. Bennet rubbed his hands together and laughed. "Soon she shall be gone — and I shall be able to read in peace!"

Mr. Bennet sat in his armchair and the family cat hopped into his lap to be petted. Mr. Bennet stroked the cat's white fur as he laughed. "Bwu ha ha ha ha ha! I shall make Lydia marry him. And then she will be gone. Mwu hahahaha."

It is at this time that a fashionable gentleman strolls into our tale wearing Miss Lydia's favorite aphrodisiac: A red officer's coat tailored so that it stuck to the body and showed off every curve of the fine male figure. The price of this coat had been placed onto the credit of our gentleman, and he never intended to repay the tailor who had lovingly produced such a fine coat for such a fine looking gentleman. In fact this gentleman believed that the tailor had been amply recompensed for his work by the chance to make clothes for him.

Yes! It is Mr. Wickham!

Mr. Wickham did meet the Bennet sisters upon the road. And Mr. Collins had walked them into Meryton, incessantly plying his attentions upon Lydia who happily ignored him. To increase his love for her by suspense, Mr. Collins approvingly became more convinced of her affections the less attention she paid to him. By this point she affected to not even hear him when he spoke to her. A more certain sign of desperate passion could *not* be imagined.

However, in our tale Wickham first discovers his place at Mrs. Phillip's card party that night.

For as circumstances happened, when he met the group upon the road, Elizabeth was not there! For she and Mr. Darcy were in Mr. Bennet's study arguing (very quietly) about their opinions on the competing merits of modern novelists. As they conversed Mr. Bennet happily read his book and compulsively petted his white cat. Elizabeth thought Mr. Darcy's opinions upon the book they were discussing were intelligent, well spoken, and even clever, but still illustrated yet further his terrible character, as proven by his finding her not handsome enough for his ~~very handsome person~~ excessively noble featured and tall person.

At the precise moment Mr. Wickham greeted her sisters with his easy and gentlemanlike charm, Darcy confessed his deepest secret to Elizabeth: He *actually* liked *Pamela* even though it completely misunderstood the nature of the upper classes of society, was melodramatic, was moralistic, and was not clever. Even though she despised the novel, and Darcy (of course), it was impossible for Elizabeth not to be moved and touched by his entrusting such a dark and disgraceful secret to her.

Perhaps his features were not *too* noble for her to admire. Thus when Mr. Bingley rode through Meryton that morning, he was not turned back by Darcy's disgust at meeting Mr. Wickham, and thus he too received an invitation to the card party shouted decorously from Mrs. Phillip's upstairs window. He of course happily accepted so that he might spend more time with the angelically beautiful Miss Bennet. In their worry regarding the state of their brother's attachment to the unfortunately beautiful Miss Bennet, Bingley's sisters attended the card party as well, despite their distaste for being suppered and card gamed by the wife of a country lawyer. Darcy did not attend. He had become deeply concerned that despite her lack of dowry and her poor connections, and her odorous cousin, he was in some danger from Miss Elizabeth. He should no longer pay so much attention to her dark gleaming eyes, sparkling wit, and mischievous tongue — mmmmm her tongue. She could do so many things with her tongue.

No! Ungentlemanly! Do not think such things, Darcy. That is an improper licentious thought about a fine young lady! Stop it! Stop! Present at the card party likewise was the stooped and manly figure of Mr. Collins: our unbathed, Falstaffian (in proportions, though not morals), and ill-dressed hero. But he plays no significant part in this evening, as he spent the entire time talking to Lovely Cousin Lydia.

Miss Lydia spent the first half of the evening in increasing frustration as she pretended he wasn't there and she chattered happily to the officers. But at some point during the course of the night, she decided having such an unshakeable admirer spoke well for her consequence. And he really didn't smell that bad once you got used to him. She started to smile at Mr. Collins's remarks, even as she mostly continued to ignore him in favor of her red coated, yet often awkward and pimply young warriors.

Mr. Wickham immediately approached Miss Bingley upon his arrival at the party, and as Mr. Bingley was occupied with Jane, he introduced himself to her.

She sneered.

Mr. Wickham's coat was clearly not made by one of the most exclusive tailors though it fit him exceeding well. Mr. Wickham made several further sallies and attempts to gain her favor and attention. She wanted to ignore him. He was penniless, and she did not prattle with penniless gentlemen. However, Miss Caroline Bingley had gone to some of the most exclusive preparatory schools in London, and thus it was not possible for her to be directly rude to someone who she was directly speaking to — though she was expert at hiding subtle sallies against them that no one but a person of fashionable and discerning character, such as herself, could ever notice. And as Mr. Wickham assiduously paid court to her fortune of twenty thousand pounds a year, and her station as the wealthiest single woman in the neighborhood, something changed between them while they conversed the card party away: they discovered, through entirely accidental moments of candidness that became more intentional over time, that they thought alike on everything.

Mr. Wickham liked to simper and agree with those who were socially above him. She liked to simper and agree with those socially above *her*, like Mr. Darcy and his relations! They were just the same!

They both thought Mr. Darcy was odiously pompous, and his sister was an excessively sensitive bore.

His dearest desire, he confessed to her, was to marry a rich woman who was in the highest social circles. Her dearest desire was to marry a rich man who travelled in the highest circles. They were just the same, again!

They both loved clothes, and thought that orange was an excellent color on a woman, and that feathers improved every hat. He liked to gamble, and she liked to gamble as well — he lost a great deal of money to her that night, which he could not pay, being penniless.

Neither of them ever had enough money. They were just the same! Once more!

In fact Miss Bingley had never felt so understood as she did during those glowing happy hours of conversation with Mr. Wickham, and he had never felt so in tune with the mind of a woman.

He happily whistled an indecent ditty as he returned to his lodgings that night: Miss Caroline Bingley was just like a rich female version of himself.

The following day after breakfast Mr. Collins sought out Lydia in the drawing room where she was quite busy threading a new ribbon into the straw bonnet she had worn the first day. He begged, pressing a hand into his ample bosom, for the chance to kiss her hand, for it was the most delicate and perfect hand in the world entire, and he could then die happily, having touched his lips against it. Just as Israel said unto his son Joseph that he could die happily having seen his son lived yet.

Mr. Collins said that, and many of the other little compliments that he passed time devising for the entertainment of Lovely Lydia.

"La! You are so dull. But you are such a joke. I like that you follow me around so — but I shall never love anyone but an officer!"

Mr. Collins now began to understand the true nature of her objection to his person. And it was a most difficult problem, for his benefactoress had no patronage in the army, and he had been trained for his profession of the church. But surely this could not truly be such a serious objection in the sublime mind of Lovely Lydia?

"Come here!" Lydia exclaimed, holding her bonnet out to him. "Lizzy is not here and I must see how it looks upon another person." And so saying, she made Mr. Collins to wear her bonnet and had him turn about until he felt quite dizzy so she could study its appearance from each side. Then she reached down (for she was taller than he), and retrieved the bonnet from his head. "Ugh! Your hair got grease on my bonnet. Heavens, take a bath!"

And thus Mr. Collins was thrown into the Dark Night of the Soul, as his two greatest passions — that for Lovely Lydia and that for obeying Lady Catherine — were thrown into deepest opposition. His paternal patroness disapproved of bathing. His lovely love wished him to bathe.

His patroness. His Goddess.

Lovely Lydia. Lady Catherine de Bourgh.

Bath. No bath.

Mr. Collins stumbled outside, walking the frigid rain soaked lanes around Meryton on that cold winter day for many hours as he pondered upon this impossible question, and the difficulty of devising an answer, of choosing what was dearest in his heart, for until then obeying Lady Catherine and desiring Lovely Lydia had followed together in his mind, for *She* had commanded him to go amongst his cousins and choose a wife from amongst *them*. That is *She* had commanded him to choose *Her* — I should note at this point that though our hero, Mr. Collins, had lapsed into idolatrous thoughts and now placed creature above creator, this should not be held against him, for though he was a clergyman, he was not fit for such a holy profession, being such a heroic lover.

The next days likewise, until the night of the Netherfield ball, Mr. Collins struggled with this heavy burden upon his soul. On the night of the Netherfield ball he was still undecided, and he miserably sat in an armchair next to the fire, and ignored the requests to join the party as they bundled out into the carriage, until they left him alone to contemplate the deepest dilemma a man could face: The question of love or duty.

And then our hero chose.

Two hours after the ball at Netherfield began, the door to the ballroom was hurled open.

He the bloated toad of Hunsford town swaggered into the ballroom, and it seemed all paused, even the music, to look upon him.

And then, with a thunderous trip over a false step right past the doors of the room, he fell flat onto the floor. And thus our waddling, sweat soaked, fat clad and *bathed* champion arrived at the Netherfield Ball.

"I'm all right! I'm all right!" He leapt to his feet. "Lydia! Lovely Cousin Lydia! You must dance the next with me. I am clean!"

"You bathed!" Lydia looked at him with shock. "But I thought Lady Catherine ordered you never to bathe."

"Your perfection, your loveliness, your commands are of more weight to me than those of my noble patroness, Lovely, lovely Lydia. Will you now dance with me?"

She looked from side to side wildly. "Oh, officers. Officers? Where is an officer? I need an officer to distract me from this strange passion growing inside!" — she found one and pointed at him — "You, you shall dance with me."

"But you have already been asked to a set. It would be against the forms for me to dance with you, if you refuse him."

"Yes!" Mr. Collins hurried up next to them, smiling, and smelling like a baby cleaned with expensive scented soap. "You must dance with me, Lovely Cousin Lydia."

Lydia looked at him for a long time, with her mouth slightly open, and some powerful emotion roiled in her eyes. Then she looked upon the officer, and upon his redcoat. She let out several agitated huffs of breath. "Redcoats. Redcoats. Just redcoats. I am determined to only dance with redcoats." She tilted her head and said to the officer, "Did you hear that? I believe there was just a tinkling of bells. But I heard no request for my hand at dance."

Mr. Denny shrugged, decided that even if singular, it was no business of his if she offended her cousin, and Lydia was a lively girl, and he took her out to the line of the dance.

Left behind was Mr. Collins, oddly smiling as he watched her lovely lines and legs and heard the ache of the vibrating violins.

Elsewhere in the room Mr. Wickham and Miss Bingley danced every dance without break.

This was the supper dance, during which Darcy claimed the set Elizabeth had promised him. But rather than talking upon books (in a ballroom!) both their heads were full of something else. Specifically the way that Mr. Wickham and Miss Bingley ignored every convention to dance unstoppingly with each other. Clearly an engagement should be expected from them, or Mr. Bingley should do something to get the penniless officer away from his sister.

"It is a shocking pairing," Elizabeth said to Darcy after they had danced for half a minute. "I would not have expected her to shower attention on a man lacking..." She paused, not wanting to crudely say that she thought Miss Bingley was purely mercenary. "A man lacking a settled home."

Darcy smirked at her. "That was politely said. But everyone must think their apparent attachment is odd and worrisome."

"Worrisome? She has money enough for the both of them, and if she finds happiness in a charming and well-mannered man, I don't see why anyone should say them nay. Your presumptuousness, which I have castigated you for many a time this past month, shows once more."

"You think it is only my presumption that makes me dislike the match?"

"You so chuse," Elizabeth said decidedly, "that all those connected with you are well connected themselves. Isn't the town's tattle that he was your steward's son? That would be rather low for the wife of a particular friend."

"Miss Bingley is not a particular friend!"

Elizabeth giggled at his testiness. She also liked hearing him disclaim interest in another woman. "Not handsome enough to tempt you?"

"She is handsome enough," Mr. Darcy replied absentmindedly. "Though her fortune is not large enough to be worthy of note and the gold being touched by trade makes her rather low for my hand. What I dislike mainly is her — Why are you frowning at me so?"

Elizabeth didn't deign to deliver a reply. So it was not women in general that he found too unhandsome for him, just her in particular. She studied the dancing couple. Elizabeth decided she was more smartly (though cheaply) dressed, with better taste, and with a prettier face than Miss Bingley's. Elizabeth knew she only dimpled on one side, and her nose twisted off slightly more to the left, and there were a few other failures of perfect symmetry.

But next to Miss Bingley! Ha!

No accounting for taste — bad taste. Mr. Darcy's bad taste. She really wished he liked her. *No, bad thought, Lizzy. He is odious and pompous and it is good he doesn't like you.*

Mr. Darcy misinterpreted her anger. "I see you take Mr. Wickham's side, many women are taken in by his charm and looks, but I know your good sense well enough to be firmly convinced that should you have a lengthy acquaintanceship with him, your clear mind will come to see him as I do." Elizabeth half bitterly smiled. "So you do appreciate my *mind*."

"It is your chiefest charm," he replied seriously.

God! He could be so obtuse. Elizabeth looked at Mr. Darcy and shook her head. She could no longer stay angry with him, for he had somehow become a dear friend. "A woman wishes to be complimented on something other than just her cleverness."

"Then your fine eyes are your chiefest charm," he replied firmly and immediately.

They both blushed.

When their conversation continued, Mr. Darcy said, "Mr. Wickham is a fortune hunter."

Elizabeth laughed in reply, "Just because he solely seeks the company of the wealthiest woman in the neighborhood while being penniless himself, you think the worst, but — " Elizabeth paused, and the laughter entirely left her voice. "I see by your face your objection to Mr. Wickham is more particular."

"It is. He is a man of low character, and he imposed terribly on my family once, and he has given ample proof that he behaves either as a seducer or a fortune hunter."

"And now he imposes upon Miss Bingley."

"He does yet — " Darcy adopted a most confused expression, that of a man who had just been obliged by his hosts to eat a roasted scorpion while travelling in an exotic land, and who then found to his horror that he really liked the taste. "He does not."

"He does, and yet he does not. That clears up the matter entirely." Elizabeth smirked at him, and poked her tongue out to press the edge of her lips.

"It is a matter of some confusion to me." Darcy shrugged. He looked at Mr. Wickham and Miss Bingley. "I ought to separate them — I truly ought. And I did speak to her about his character. I did not tell her the details, I had no need — she claimed to be entirely convinced that he only wishes to court her for her fortune and position, but she claims that their connection is simply one of comradeship, because at last, for the first time in her life, she has met a man who is just like her and who truly understands." Darcy shuddered.

"Is that truly so terrible?"

"You surely noticed that she wishes to marry me."

"Ah! You mean to suggest she is a fortune hunter. Just like him."

"In a word. But this similarity goes deeper. And she is the sister of my friend. Even though she claims to know what she is about, and even though she is of age, and even though… my place to disrupt them. But since they met, she no longer showers me with unwanted attention, but rather spends the day entire sitting next to the window sighing softly."

"That is a sign of a worrisome attachment."

"I like the silence."

"Just like Papa," Elizabeth giggled.

"I hope I am not *that much* a misanthrope." Darcy grinned back at her smiling face.

She sighed. Both Miss Bingley and Wickham, and Jane and Mr. Bingley made fine looking couples. Happy marriages. She wished Darcy admired her for more than her mind. Elizabeth saw Mr. Collins following Lydia around the dance floor, and she thought, uncharitably, that at least they would never make a match of it.

"What brings that frown? And is there anything I might do to relieve your anxiety?"

Elizabeth looked into his deep eyes. She confessed the truth. "I have been so frightened of late for my father."

"Frightened?"

"My father. He was not always like this. I am frightened he shall force my sister to marry Mr. Collins." At Mr. Darcy's thoughtful frown, Elizabeth hurriedly added, "I never imagined he would ever make any of us marry. He always enjoyed his books, and preferred a good deal of solitude. But since his illness... he became first obsessed with noise. And then reading *all* of the books."

Mr. Darcy smiled. "It does sound like a noble endeavor."

Elizabeth giggled, and smiled at him gratefully. She knew him well enough by now that he spoke in that manner to cheer her from her anxiety, and not to dismiss her worries. "From too much good," she replied, "you can also find evil."

"Very wise." Darcy flashed a shining grin at her. "You are a woman who can find a way to say things in the middle of a ball that will be passed down to future generations with the force of a proverb."

Elizabeth helplessly laughed at his teasing. How had she ever thought he wasn't really handsome? Even if he did think she was not handsome himself, that didn't mean he couldn't tempt her. Oh yes. She was supposed to be angry at him. Oh yes. Angry. Elizabeth unconsciously licked her lips as she looked at Mr. Darcy's.

He smiled back at her, as they turned in the complicated figures of the dance.

She nervously said, "Papa's fever was so high. I really did begin to believe he might leave us. Mama had been convinced he would die. I am so happy Papa lived. I love him so much, and in his body he is healthy. But he just... he just is not the same. And he will force Lydia to marry Mr. Collins. I have heard him say so a dozen times. And I...I don't know what to do."

"He loves you. And all his daughters. He must love you more than he loves his... silence and books." Darcy's voice trailed away. It was clear from his frown that he did not believe what he said either.

They both sighed.

"Most likely this oath will never be required," Mr. Darcy said with his resonant and manly voice, "but I swear, Elizabeth — Miss Elizabeth — I swear I will do anything it takes to rescue your sister from Mr. Collins's hand." The song ended, but Mr. Darcy, seemingly unconsciously and automatically, kept her hand as he added softly, "So you see, you need not worry on any account."

During the course of the entire ball, Mr. Wickham and Caroline Bingley did in fact dance every dance, and during the course of the second half of the evening, after all involved had imbibed a great quantity of Bingley's wine and song, Wickham asked her to marry him no less than three times.

"You only ask me, as I have a fortune."

"I would make an effort to seduce you no matter how poor you were."

Miss Bingley fluttered and flushed at that reply. "You are such a sweet man."

"I am a man in love. Entirely and completely in love."

"You are not."

"Maybe not, but I want to secure your companionship, your friendship — if you were poor, I would not abandon you after I seduced you, but set you up somewhere that I could visit regularly to speak with you. For you are the only person, man or woman, I have ever met who truly understood me, who I can truly be myself with. That is more important than finding an heiress with thirty thousand pounds, or with an older and more settled family."

"You are desperate enough to take *half* my twenty thousand! — *And* we *are* a respectable family from the North of England!"

Mr. Wickham raised one eyebrow.

"Whose wealth came from trade. Yes, yes, yes. I know."

"It is unlikely you shall ever make a splendid match, so you should prefer a companionate one. Look at Mr. Darcy. Besotted by Miss Elizabeth. He is not going to marry you." Both sneered at the couple. Wickham and Miss Bingley hated them for their good looks, good luck, and good roles as the good protagonists in the novel whilst they were relegated to the role of polite villains.

Mr. Darcy and Elizabeth, dancing for a second time, paid no attention to the attention paid to them.

"I can do better than *you*."

"But you never shall find another man whose brain is as vicious and low, and quite as mad inside as your own." Miss Bingley sighed, for she knew that to be true.

"Caroline, marry me. Make me the happiest possessor of an heiress with twenty thousand pounds in the world. For I swear I shall be far happier than every other fortune hunter in England."

"Oh! Mr. Wickham!" She swooningly sighed. "If only I could."

"You can, you are of age, and I bribed one of your servants to bring me a copy of old Mr. Bingley's will. You have complete control over your own fortune."

"You bribed a servant to learn about me!" she replied bright eyed. "I never even winked at the old man's will myself!"

"Then you will marry me."

"Oh… if only…"

She paused a long time. Mr. Wickham prompted her, "If only what…"

"If only you were not an officer. It is too unsettled of a life. I will never marry an officer."

As soon as she said that, walking past them, having given up ignoring Mr. Collins, Miss Lydia Bennet shouted at her follower, "I shall only ever marry an officer!"

Together, staring at them, and entirely unprompted by the other, Mr. Wickham and Miss Bingley said together, "What ill-bred people, the Bennets." They looked at each other and laughed again.

Miss Bingley added, "But it is the well-bred ones I despise the most. Miss Eliza and Miss Jane. I don't suppose anything can be done anymore to prevent *that* disaster of a marriage."

Mr. Wickham shrugged. He rather liked to look at Jane, and liked the idea of his future brother's wife being so attractive. And he *was* determined to bring Caroline to her senses and convince her to marry him. "I can quit my commission."

"But then you would be entirely without employment. No! If I were to marry a man who was not a gentleman with his own estate, it would only be a clergyman. Those in law or trade are too unrespectable, and I will *not* let you do nothing at all. Your hands are too devilish for them to get the extra incentive to deviltry from idleness."

She wagged her finger in his face.

Mr. Wickham shot forward his head, and pretended to try to bite her finger. Miss Bingley laughed again, but then sighed. Mr. Wickham sighed as well. But his eyes lit upon Mr. Collins following Lydia Bennet, who now had begun to shyly glance back at our sausagey hero, and the beginning of an idea came to him.

The next morning Mr. Collins made a declaration of marriage to Lydia in the breakfast room. *This* declaration was made in front of the entire family, including Mr. Bennet who read through the whole thing. Mrs. Bennet did not participate in clearing the room, as she still thought Mr. Collins should pick Lizzy instead. This declaration also was considerably more impassioned than that in our dear novel.

However it ended similarly, when Mr. Collins assured Lydia that she could not actually be serious in her refusal, as his position in life was too good.

Mr. Bennet exclaimed to Lydia, when she tried to run away, "You shall marry Mr. Collins! I order you to, as your father." She stuck her lovely tongue back out at her old man. "No I won't."

"Yes you will."

"No I won't. I have solemnly sworn to only marry an officer."

"I shall lock you in your room. You shall eat nothing but books and water until you change your mind."

"I can't eat books."

"Then *read* them," replied Mr. Bennet severely. He had her taken up to her room by two footmen, and he threw several books into the room after her. Books which he had multiple copies of downstairs.

The door slammed shut on Lydia Bennet with a satisfying thud.

Mr. Collins was miserable. He understood the problem: He was not an officer.

He walked out of the house, stumblingly, unable to hear any voices that spoke to him. His life was empty, pointless, sad. He had no appetite, he could not eat (when normally he ate a great deal), he could not think, he could not even make pompous speeches upon the goodness of his benefactress. He *needed* her: Her maturity, and her intelligence. Her well moderated spirits, and her aesthetic and emotional perfection. Mr. Collins would do *anything* to marry her. But he had no sense of *what* anything would succeed at bringing him to his heart's desire. And then he heard behind him a voice of an acquaintance in the neighborhood calling out his name.

Elizabeth immediately went to her father when he returned to his study after breakfast. "Papa, you can't do this. You must release Lydia. You must. You are not being yourself. You love us, I would have never believed that you would try to force one of your daughters into such an obviously unbalanced match. Do not do this."

"Lizzy," he replied, lowering his book at last with an air of great frustration. "Can you not see that I am reading John Farley's treatise on the General View of the Agriculture and Minerals of Derbyshire: With Observations On the Means of Their Improvement? Your friend Darcy lent it to me."

"My friend?"

"Yes *your* friend. Do you think I haven't noticed you two constantly talking about books when you sit together in my domain? I can see you like him very much, and I approve of any young man who reads as much as he does, and who has an extensive library which he is willing to lend to me from. I will give him my hearty assent if he ever asks it. You can tell him that, and he won't need to bother with interrupting me from reading long enough to ask my consent."

Elizabeth blushed. Surely not. Surely not.

Her father was quite mad, and here was more proof of it. They were just friends. Just friends. And he was pompous, and quite arrogant still. And thought her unhandsome.

"Lydia, Papa. You must release her, Papa."

"I shall do no such thing until she agrees to marry Mr. Collins."

"Surely you don't think they would be happy."

"I do not see why not, he is able to read, whatever his other ample deficits are, and she cannot. She should marry a man who can read."

"I am sure Lydia can read."

"Oh." Mr. Bennet replied in a skeptical tone. After a long pause he added, "Have you ever seen her to do so, for I have not."

Elizabeth searched her mind, and realized that she could not ever recall seeing her sister read. Good God, was Lydia illiterate? How had she never known? Was she a terrible sister? She should have taken a hand in her upbringing. And her Papa even more so.

"Papa, if she cannot read — and I am still not certain that she can't — 'tis a failure of her education. A matter *you* should have redressed. It would be wrong to punish her on such a matter."

"I was just reading in the book about sheep rot. It is a disease in the hooves of sheep that is common in Derbyshire when they are allowed to wander in wet fields for graze. You can manage it by carving the diseased material away and tying cotton pads to the bottom of the hoofs."

"Papa! Your daughters are more important than your books!"

He blinked at her and shook his head. And he then blinked again. "I am sorry, for a moment I thought your mother was here."

Elizabeth wanted to scream at him. She stomped up and grabbed the book from him and shut it firmly. With a loud thud she slammed it on the desk.

"I borrowed that book," he whined.

"Let. Lydia. Go."

"No! Soon she shall be gone, gone, gone. Never to bother me with her noise again. And then I shall be free! Free! Free to read *all* the books! I shall read *all* the books before I die." Mr. Bennet's eyes bulged out and he tilted his head back and began a long cackling laugh. "Free of the noise, Mwuhahahahahahahaha."

As he laughed, their completely white cat ran into the room from somewhere and drawn by the sound jumped onto Mr. Bennet's lap. Mr. Bennet happily stroked its fur as he crazily continued to laugh, before he at last settled down, pulled the book back to him, searched out his place again and continued to read.

Elizabeth watched horrified, seeing that everything she had feared was come to pass.

Her father had lost his mind. He had passed round the bend. He had thrown out several cards from his deck. Bats were in his belfry, and though a candle was lit in the window, no one was home. His book was missing both the table of contents and the index. In a word: Insane.

The first attempt she made to resolve matters was by seeking medical expertise for her father's serious condition. "Mr. Jones, Mr. Jones. You must do something to help my father. You must."

"Oh!" The apothecary said worriedly, "What is the matter with him? He appeared to be in the best of health when I saw him last. Much younger and more vigorous appearing than I am, and we are of an age."

"He has lost his mind. Maybe some poultice or infusion will help him."

"Lost his mind!"

"He cackles endlessly about reading all of the books. He is obsessed with getting rid of noise, and he intends to force Lydia to marry Mr. Collins."

"Oh. That's all? I thought you worried about something serious."

"This *is* serious."

"Such a humorous situation, there is nothing to help. Now if you had come to me with a problem about his humerus I could help you." Mr. Jones laughed with bright eyes, rocking his head back and forth, at his own pun — though Elizabeth was not at all certain it deserved even that low appellation.

"Of course he hates noise. Any reasonable man would despise the racket a full family of women make. I'm surprised he ever let you all talk."

Elizabeth wanted to strangle the apothecary. "If you were a real medical man, a doctor," she snapped, "you would see the seriousness of the situation."

"Useless fellows. They'd just bleed him because he was too sane to be healthy. Your father is lucky there is no real doctor in the neighborhood. I wonder if I could get him to match Miss Kitty with my son. Her dowry would not be so bad for us..."

Elizabeth threw up her hands and left his place of business, still too well-mannered to hurl the door shut behind her as she wanted to.

Mr. Jones would be of no use. Although his son was a fetching young lad, and quite industrious. Kitty could do worse.

Elizabeth stepped out into the thin winter sun. She looked up and down the road, almost frantic.

What to do? What to do? What to do? She must at least save Lydia from such a grotesque and horrible marriage. And in the distance she saw the smokestacks of Netherfield merrily puffing. And she remembered there was one man who had promised to help if she needed it. One man who she could trust.

Elizabeth squared her shoulders and marched down the familiar road.

As she passed the inn on the way out of town, she saw from the corner of her eye the mismatched pair of the handsome Mr. Wickham and the... rather less handsome Mr. Collins talking in the common room with a pair of empty pitchers of beer between them.

Naturally, upon her arrival Darcy was eager to provide every help that Elizabeth might need. For completely disinterested reasons. Naturally.

Their plan was simple: A little before dawn they would put a ladder against Lydia's window. The ladder would be muffled with felt, so as to not wake Mr. Bennet, but their deepest worry was that Mr. Bennet was so sensitive to noise at this date that he would be able to hear any sound they might make, no matter how soft. They would take Lydia in Darcy's carriage to London to be hidden at the Gardiners until such time as Mr. Bennet regained his sanity, though as Mr. Darcy observed, it was quite likely that Mr. Bennet would be satisfied with an unmarried Lydia living in London, so long as she was not present to disturb *his* studies.

Upon her return home Elizabeth looked up at Lydia's window, closed and bolted against cold winter. Lydia was her sister, and though she did not like her much, she loved her nevertheless. Elizabeth whispered her vow, "I will save you from our father."

When Elizabeth went outside a little before dawn to meet Darcy, who muscularly carried a long ladder without aid, she was surprised to see a candle burning in Lydia's window. It was good that she was still awake, so that they would not need to make noise waking her up, but Elizabeth worriedly wondered what horrible thoughts and fears were going through her sister's mind to keep her from her sleep.

They settled the ladder against the window, and waited, worried that the noise would draw Mr. Bennet, and hoping it would draw Lydia to her window.

There was no sound from the house.

Elizabeth and Mr. Darcy shared a look. Her heart hammered nervously.

She nodded at her friend, gestured for him to hold the ladder, and climbed up to Lydia's window. Elizabeth knocked on it softly, but Lydia made no response. Elizabeth peered through the window. A brief thought passed through her mind that maybe Lydia had climbed out from the window and gone to ground and made her own escape, and now could be anywhere.

But no!

Lydia sat on her bed cross legged with a book that she gazed at raptly in her lap, and an almost burnt to the nub candle next to her.

Elizabeth gaped in surprise at the sight. Lydia *did* know how to read!

Then why had she never done so before?

Not now. Elizabeth shook the question away. She knocked harder on the window.

No response from the diligently reading girl.

Elizabeth hissed at the window.

No response again. But then Lydia started laughing uproariously and closed the book over her finger to keep the place as she laughed and laughed. Elizabeth recognized the cover, and knew she was reading *Evelina*.

How had Elizabeth's life come to this?

It was quite cold. It was almost December, and even in her coat the late night freeze seeped through her clothes, and Lydia, who they were come to rescue, ignored them to laugh and have a grand time. In her anger Elizabeth half forgot her fear of waking her father and banged softly on the window.

At last Lydia looked up and came to window and opened it. "Why are you making such a racket! Can't you see I'm reading? At last I understand why Papa is always so mad."

"For God's sake! We are here to rescue you."

"Oh." She seemed stumped by that for a minute. "Come back when I'm done with the book."

Elizabeth gripped the ladder so hard her knuckles turned white. *Don't scream. Don't scream. That will bring Papa.* "Why don't you come down now, Lyddie? You must be hungry; we have food in the carriage."

The girl looked tempted. And she touched her stomach with the hand not holding her book. Then a resolution fell upon Lydia. She shook her fist in Elizabeth's face. "Knowledge and an excellent plot are more important than *food*! You of all women, being such a great reader, should know *that*!"

Don't scream.

Elizabeth's hand shot out and she snatched the book from Lydia's hand.

The girl screeched in outrage. "What was that for, Lizzy!"

"You can read in the carriage."

Elizabeth quickly climbed down the ladder, and Lydia followed muttering under her breath, without bothering to put on anything warmer.

Mr. Darcy raised his eyebrows when Lydia snatched back the book from Elizabeth the instant her slippered foot touched the cold ground, and ignoring the weather and the way she started to shiver, immediately flipped through the book to find her place once more. They had to guide her as they walked to the carriage, because she immediately began reading again as she walked.

"Well." Darcy smiled at Elizabeth. "Off to London. You me, Lydia, and Evelina. It is a quite good book."

The carriage started off. Lydia did not seem to notice anything for the first five minutes of their travel with her nose in the book. Then she sniffed, without looking up. "What is that smell?"

Mr. Darcy pulled the basket out of its compartment. "I had the cook at Netherfield prepare something for our breakfast."

"Excellent," Lydia replied. She grabbed the basket with her free hand, shook it until a pastry fell out onto Darcy's velvet cushions, grabbed for it, smearing some of the fruit jam into the blue seat cover, and then began to munch, all without taking her eyes off the book.

She reached the end of her page, she stuffed the rest of the pasty into her mouth, and then wiped her fingers off on the cushions, carefully cleaning them, before changing the page. Elizabeth burned with embarrassment, but then Darcy caught her eye and smirked, and both of them began to laugh uproariously. Lydia complained loudly about not knowing the joke, and demanded they stop so she could concentrate on reading

Five miles from Longbourn, the sound of clattering hooves in pursuit came up behind them. Lydia was too absorbed in the book to care, but Darcy frowned. "I had hoped your father would not pursue us."

Elizabeth grabbed his hand. "Do promise you will not allow him to lock Lydia up once more."

"Do not worry." He smiled softly at her.

The horseman pulled up in front of the carriage and forced them to stop.

It was not Mr. Bennet.

Rather the sweat soaked and fat clad hero of our tale: Mr. Collins!

He wore a fine red coat that was many sizes too small for himself, and when he tried to dismount, he fell onto his knees, and every button on the coat popped open, and two of them popped off. He stood up, brushing the dust from his pants.

"Lovely Cousin Lydia!" he cried into the carriage.

At last! Something that made Lydia put down the book. She looked up at Mr. Collins's voice. And she stared and gaped, taking in his red coat, and the officer's sword at his side, that nearly tripped him once more, and the fine white belt over his chest.

She stepped from the carriage, her eyes wide. "Mr. Collins."
"Lovely Lydia! I have switched places with Mr. Wickham. He shall take my parish, and I his commission. I now am an officer. Will you marry me!"
Lydia looked him up and down, pale faced. "You... you did *that* for me? That much."
"Oh, Lovely Lydia, I would do anything for you!"
"My hero! My Mr. Collins!" And so saying Lydia swooned into his arms, and they began to passionately kiss.
Elizabeth pressed her hand over her mouth, incapable of making any sense of what she was watching.
Her jaw fell further open as she watched Lydia and Mr. Collins first toss off his red coat, and following that they worked his inner shirt off, displaying the ample folds of skin, and the black cross of hair on his chest.
It was a grotesque sight and Elizabeth turned away in disgust. But maybe this was a good thing, if Lydia was happy...
Elizabeth shuddered and forced herself to keep from vomiting.
Mr. Darcy looked at her rather than the shirtless fat man and his fiancée groping each other openly in the middle of the road.
He smiled warmly at her. Elizabeth fluttered in her stomach. There was meaning in his gaze.
To break the tension she quipped, "At least Lydia shall not be *forced* to marry Mr. Collins."
Mr. Darcy laughed, his eyes bright, his face clear, and his smile easy and handsome.
He looked at her with good humor and happiness shining in his eyes. "It seems marriage is in the air here in Hertfordshire. Dearest Elizabeth, will you accept my hand and make me the happiest of men?"

Epilogue

There was quite a group of happy couples to marry in the neighborhood of Meryton over the following month: Mr. Wickham to Miss Bingley, after Lady Catherine was charmed by Wickham into approving of him as her new clergyman; Jane and Bingley, naturally; Elizabeth to Mr. Darcy; and of course the hero of our tale at last took into his large deserving bosom his beloved image of maturity and perfection, Miss Lydia Bennet.

Not everyone was so happy at these nuptials.

Mary Bennet had been infatuated with Mr. Darcy, and upon her sister's marriage she took to wearing black and writing dark poetry. Poetry that mixed images of death with complaints about how she was entirely misunderstood by everyone, especially her family and friends. Eventually she submitted her poems to a publisher, hoping to become the female Byron.

But alas, those publishers also misunderstood her.

Kitty in turn had a tendre towards our over plump hero. She never explained why, but she refused to speak to her entirely unbothered and, in fact, unnoticing sister for six months.

Jane and Bingley married by special license as soon as Bingley returned from his trip to London. He was unaccompanied on his return to Netherfield by his sister who, now that Mr. Wickham was a clergyman, was busy with him anticipating their wedding vows.

Darcy and Elizabeth instead followed the sedate route of having the banns published.

The establishment of so many children, in such a short space of time, produced so happy an effect in Mrs. Bennet's character as to make her a sensible, amiable and well-informed woman for the rest of her years.

Mr. Bennet, however, never recovered. Fortunately for him his wife no longer was so nervous, and learned to manage all the business of the estate on her own, leaving him to pursue his endless quest of reading *all* the books.

Their many, many grandchildren would always know him as the crazy old man who sat in an armchair in the library, with a book open on the stand in front of him, as he cackled while stroking a white cat.

The End

Afterward

Bits of this idea have bounced around in the back of my head for around three years now, and last year before I finished work on *Too Gentlemanly* I wrote the first three thousand words of this before being not sure what to write next. After the rather decidedly modest success of the fantasy novel I wrote in the middle of this year I decided to return to my beloved and loving JAFF and when I found the part of this story that I'd already written, I laughed the whole time. It was almost as though that section had been written by someone with exactly my sense of humor...

The first part of this book is almost entirely unchanged from what I had written then. I was scared to mess with what clearly worked, at least for me.

The rest flowed very quickly and easily, and now you have it. Of course my fans will want a bigger book than this, and I currently have a sixty thousand word rough draft of a new novel. Right now, I'm leaving it to sit and marinate in the back of mind for about a month and a half before returning to cook it to hoped for perfection. If any of you have read Steven King's memoir *On Writing*, letting books sit for a while between drafts is the one idea which stuck with me from that book.

The new book will be: *A Compromised Compromise*: When Elizabeth trips over a bear rug and Darcy catches her in his arms in the Netherfield library while they were arguing about Mr. Wickham during the Netherfield ball, their angry passion turns into, well, passion. They would have come to their senses and stopped kissing after a minute, of course, but Mrs. Bennet, Mr. Bingley, and Sir William Lucas just happened to pick the wrong moment to enter the rather public room they had indiscreetly secreted themselves in.

I plan to finish in November and I hope this book will be released in December, and I have three other outlines that I am interested in working on for the novel after that one. If you want to be informed when my new books come out, or when I run kindle unlimited sales on my existing books sign up for the email list: Click Here!

Also, I want to urge you to donate with me to help those suffering in extreme poverty. The world is becoming a better place, and it is possible that within our lifetimes we will see extreme poverty end. Be part of this great change. Be part of bringing medical care to those in war zones and in extreme poverty. I support Doctors Without Borders because they are an efficient and transparent organization, but there are other groups who can make your money do an enormous amount of good. So pick one, and join me in creating the future we want to see.

Finally among the P&P variations I've read in the last few months, my favorite was Renata McMann and Summer Hanford's *Hypothetically Married*. I've liked everything I've read by them. There is something about their sense of humor and how they usually use their version of Anne de Bourgh as a central PoV who watches Elizabeth and Darcy, while she has some story of her own that I just find really appealing in a fun, sweet way.

October 2018

Made in United States
North Haven, CT
18 July 2023

39217052R00032